Snake-Tacular!

BLACKBIRCH®
PRESS

THOMSON

GALE

San Diego • Detroit • New York • San Francisco • Cleveland • New Haven, Conn. • Waterville, Maine • London • Munich

© 2004 by Blackbirch Press™. Blackbirch Press™ is an imprint of The Gale Group, Inc., a division of Thomson Learning, Inc.

Blackbirch Press™ and Thomson Learning™ are trademarks used herein under license.

For more information, contact
The Gale Group, Inc.
27500 Drake Rd.
Farmington Hills, MI 48331-3535
Or you can visit our Internet site at http://www.gale.com

LIBRARY OF CONGRESS CATALOGING-IN-PUBLICATION DATA

Snake-tacular / Elaine Pascoe, book editor.
    p. cm. — (The Jeff Corwin experience)
Summary: Television personality Jeff Corwin takes the reader on an expedition around the world to investigate different varieties of snakes.
Includes bibliographical references and index.
  ISBN 1-4103-0205-9 (hardback : alk. paper) — ISBN 1-4103-0206-7 (pbk. : alk. paper)
  1. Snakes—Juvenile literature. [1. Snakes. 2. Corwin, Jeff.] I. Pascoe, Elaine. II. Corwin, Jeff. III. Series.

  QL666.O6S625 2004
  597.96—dc22   2003007522

Printed in China
10 9 8 7 6 5 4 3 2 1

Ever since I was a kid, I dreamed about traveling around the world, visiting exotic places, and seeing all kinds of incredible animals. And now, guess what? That's exactly what I get to do!

Yes, I am incredibly lucky. But, you don't have to have your own television show on Animal Planet to go off and explore the natural world around you. I mean, I travel to Madagascar and the Amazon and all kinds of really cool places—but I don't need to go that far to see amazing wildlife up close. In fact, I can find thousands of incredible critters right here, in my own backyard—or in my neighbor's yard (he does get kind of upset when he finds me crawling around in the bushes, though). The point is, no matter where you are, there's fantastic stuff to see in nature. All you have to do is look.

I love snakes, for example. Now, I've come face to face with the world's most venomous vipers—some of the biggest, some of the strongest, and some of the rarest. But I've also found an amazing variety of snakes just traveling around my home state of Massachusetts. And I've taken trips to preserves, and state parks, and national parks—and in each place I've enjoyed unique and exciting plants and animals. So, if I can do it, you can do it, too (except for the hunting venomous snakes part!). So, plan a nature hike with some friends. Organize some projects with your science teacher at school. Ask mom and dad to put a state or a national park on the list of things to do on your next family vacation. Build a bird house. Whatever. But get out there.

As you read through these pages and look at the photos, you'll probably see how jazzed I get when I come face to face with beautiful animals. That's good. I want you to feel that excitement. And I want you to remember that—even if you don't have your own TV show—you can still experience the awesome beauty of nature almost anywhere you go—any day of the week. I only hope that I can help bring that awesome power and beauty a little closer to you. Enjoy!

Best Wishes!

Jeff

Snake-Tacular

My world is filled with serpents...
and we're going to explore that
world from the rain forests of South
America, to the swamps of Louisiana,
to the deserts of Africa, and every
place in between. We'll look at some
of my favorite creatures. You guessed
it—snakes.

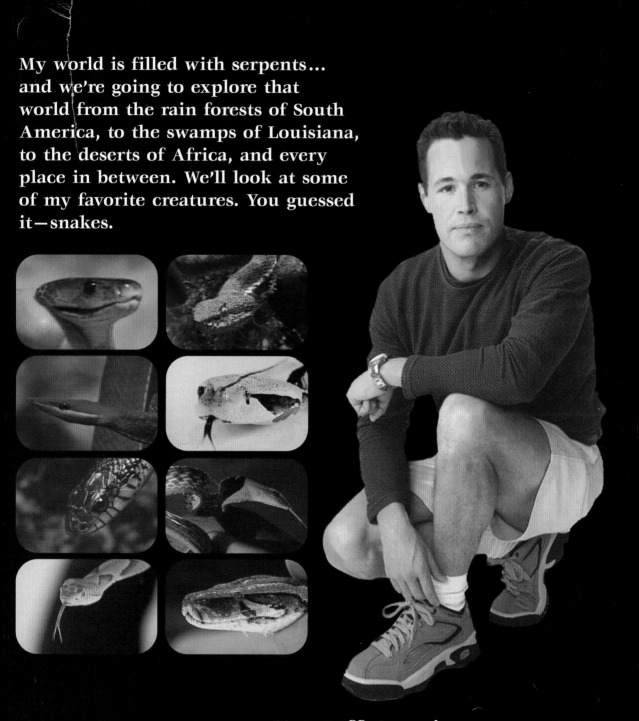

I'm Jeff Corwin.
Welcome to Snake-Tacular.

I could look at snakes all day.

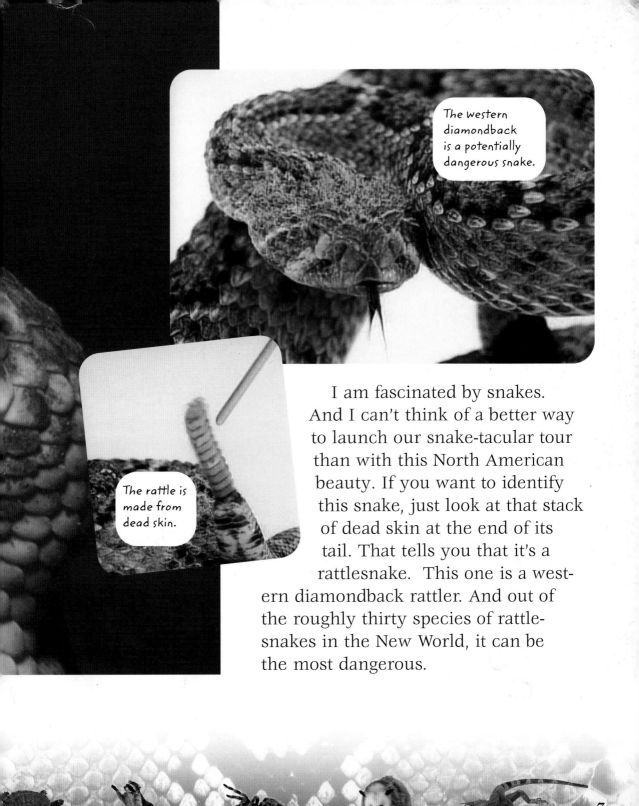

The western diamondback is a potentially dangerous snake.

The rattle is made from dead skin.

I am fascinated by snakes. And I can't think of a better way to launch our snake-tacular tour than with this North American beauty. If you want to identify this snake, just look at that stack of dead skin at the end of its tail. That tells you that it's a rattlesnake. This one is a western diamondback rattler. And out of the roughly thirty species of rattlesnakes in the New World, it can be the most dangerous.

Now this viper has a cousin that is very different in appearance, very beautiful. To find it, we have to go to a small island off the coast of Brazil....

This is Queimada Grande.

Welcome to Queimada Grande Island, in Brazil. No humans live here—and no wonder—because this island is crawling with deadly vipers. It's a four-hour boat ride from here to the mainland, and the Brazilian government requires us to bring antivenin, the medicine used for snakebites.

These vipers are tricky....

...but I've got him. A beautiful viper.

Between the leaves of this bromeliad is a beautiful snake. I need to concentrate to catch it. These vipers are very small and very quick, so they're very tricky to catch.

My gosh, this is a feisty snake! When left alone, vipers by nature like to mind their own business. The problem with these snakes is that when they're pressed or when they feel threatened, they are quick to struggle, quick to strike. I don't want to be bitten by this

These vipers are quick to strike.

snake, and I also don't want this snake to injure himself—and he could do that easily by puncturing his own flesh with those two very large fangs in the front of his mouth. I'm using my fingers to prevent that. I have my thumb and middle finger on either side of his jaw, and I have my index finger supporting his head, but he's really moving around a lot. I'm afraid he's going to injure himself, so I'm going to let him go.

By the way, although I've described how I've held this snake, that's not an instruction for you to go capture your own snake!

When they told us that this island was crawling with snakes, I really didn't believe them. But there are snakes everywhere. This one is tasting the air with his tongue, picking up our scent. I wonder what it's like be a snake with a tongue that tastes the world.

He's rattling his tail as a warning. But unlike his relative the rattlesnake, this viper doesn't have a rattle. Instead he relies on the leaves and sticks around him on the ground, flicking with his tail to make a sound when he feels alarmed. We'll let him go.

Next stop, Ecuador...

Here's a real treasure. Right in front of me, you can see a spectacular snake that's come down from the forest canopy. It's a green vine snake.

Here I am in the forest of Ecuador.

While traveling in places like India and Southeast Asia, I have captured snakes that look just like this one. It's an example of something called convergence—when two species in two different parts of the world evolve similar survival skills or adaptations to meet the challenges of the

And here's a gorgeous green vine snake.

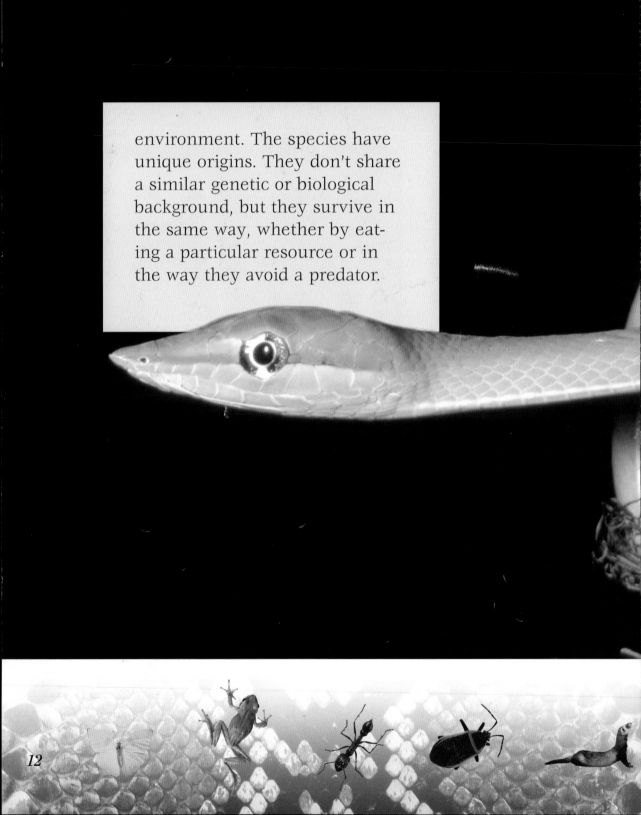

environment. The species have unique origins. They don't share a similar genetic or biological background, but they survive in the same way, whether by eating a particular resource or in the way they avoid a predator.

Vine snakes blend in with the branches on which they live.

See the snake?

Look at that leaf-shaped head.

This vine snake just hangs out here. You could walk by and never know that this was a two-meter-long snake. You would think it was the extension of a vine or a tendril of a philodendron. But it is a wonderful snake.

Now, let's head to Panama.

I picked the most inaccessible part of Panama to go snake hunting in, an area called the Darién. There are no roads; you have to fly in by chartered plane. But it's here I've found one of the most amazing-looking snakes I've ever seen.

See the scales above the eyes? Look like eyelashes...

This is an eyelash viper. Although they're not particularly aggressive, they are very, very venomous—and they have a very good reach. About a third of all viper bites are dry, meaning venom isn't delivered. But those aren't good odds in my book. That's why

Skin made of scales.

These snakes have beautiful coloring.

you have to be so careful when you're working with venomous snakes. If you screw up, you can be dead. And you can't blame the snake.

Look right above his eyes, where you can see the row of scales. That's why this snake is called the eyelash viper, not because it has hair. Reptiles don't have hair; they have scales.

And look at the camouflage. These are the prettiest vipers you'll find in the New World. They come in all sorts of colors—orange, yellow, green. This one is cinnamon. No matter how much of an unnatural fear of snakes is coiled up in your body, when you look at this creature you can't help but see a beautiful animal.

Copperheads are common snakes.

Now here's a real snake-tacular creature. Check it out—a gorgeous southern copperhead. Copperheads are probably one of the most common vipers you'll find living in North America. Next we're going to the sultry swamps of Louisiana to find a cousin of this snake.

These guys are all over North America.

I've found a baby water moccasin.

I love Louisiana because it gives us wonderful animals to discover—alligators, snapping turtles, big rattlesnakes. But here's one of my favorites, a tiny little guy only eight inches in length but armed with venom.

What we're looking at is a brand new water moccasin, probably a month old. And when a baby water moccasin comes into the world, it might be

He's little, but his venom is strong.

This little tail looks like a worm.

tiny, it might be cute, but it is producing a hemotoxin—a blood- and tissue-destroying venom— just like its parents.

In some cases, juvenile snakes can be even more venomous than adult snakes because their venom is more concentrated. Snakes use their venom to kill prey. Because young snakes are

smaller, they produce less venom. So that venom has to be potent to do the trick real fast.

When this animal is hunting, it holds very still. It has wonderful camouflage to blend in with leaves and reeds and other plant matter. And then it twitches its tail to draw in lizards, small frogs, and all sorts of smaller animals that it can prey on. It's literally using that tail as bait.

Now, on to Arizona.

These guys blend right into their surroundings. Amazing camouflage.

Don't want to slip with the black-tail rattlesnake.

Arizona is known for its deserts, but in the mountains there are some great serpents to be found. And here I've found one very cool Arizona native. I'm in a really tricky spot right here, on a steep slope, and hanging on the end of my snake stick I have one of the prettiest rattle-snakes you're going to find in the Southwest. This is the black-tail rattlesnake. With the protection of a nice long stick, I can show you that not only is the tail of this snake black, but the very tip of his muzzle is black as well.

Even though these snakes are venomous and dangerous—if you're sloppy with them and don't respect their space— they are, for the most part, not aggressive. It's not in their nature just to come out and strike you. They would much rather allow their colors to blend in with these gray and yellow rocks, and not be disturbed.

Next stop, Africa....

The Gabon viper

Just look at the girth of this snake. It's a Gabon viper, one of the fattest venomous snakes on our planet and a beautiful, beautiful animal. It's also infamous for having the longest fangs, up to two inches in length.

This creature is ovoviviparous. Try to say that ten times! Being ovoviviparous means that these snakes, instead of laying eggs, give birth to live young.

The Gabon viper is named for a country in Africa, the country of Gabon. But some snakes are named for the way they move....

The desert of Namibia, Africa, is absolutely breathtaking, and one of the strange serpents here is much better adapted to this harsh landscape than I am.

In my hands is a delicate but very venomous snake, a desert sidewinder. It's also called Peringuey's adder, but it's commonly known as a sidewinder because of the way it moves. It throws the top part of its body forward, and then the rest of the body follows in loops as it moves across the sand. Only a small part of the body touches the hot sand at one time.

See how this snake moves?

This snake moves in a unique way—it reduces contact with the hot sand.

potent bite. He is a viper and, as with most species of vipers, his venom is designed to both kill prey and destroy the tissue of the prey, to make the digestion process that much easier.

His body is brown almost to the very end, but the tip of his tail is black. He uses his tail as a lure. He twitches and dangles that lure, bringing in hungry lizards. Then he bites them, kills them with his venom, and swallows them whole.

Talk about contrast. The sand dune where that

Sidewinders pack a potent punch.

The very tip of the tail is black.

Pouncing on a black mamba— very dangerous.

Talk about contrast. The sand dune where that wonderful little sidewinder lives is only a short trip from the habitat of the black mamba, but the two snakes are light-years apart in terms of size and temperament.

The black mamba is one of the most dangerous snakes in the world, and I am in seventh heaven right now. For a herpetologist to see this creature face-to-face—it doesn't get any better than this. It's a spectacular creature when respected, and one that really brings home the beauty and the magnificence of Africa.

This snake is lightning fast—his strike is nothing but a blur. He's a member of the elapid snake family. And he's a little different because he has control over his fangs. They lie back along his jaw, and then spring forward when he's ready to bite.

I have to be very, very careful because the venom in this snake is potent. It is a neurotoxin, a venom that's designed to shut down the nervous system of his prey. If this mamba were to land a bite on me, I would have anywhere from a half hour to four hours to start receiving antivenin. If you're bitten by this snake, and you don't get the antivenin, you are going to die.

I'm holding one of the world's deadliest snakes.

When I first started to track the black mamba, I wasn't scared. But when I discovered that the government of Namibia insisted that we have an ambulance, a helicopter, and a physician standing by, that's when I started getting nervous!

Now I want you to see a snake that isn't venomous, but still is an amazing discovery.

The rainforests of Madagascar are home to a gorgeous snake, the Madagascar hognose. Why do we call this guy the hognose snake? Look at the end of his muzzle, his rostrum. You can see it is slightly curled up, like a hog's snout. The snake uses his nose like a spade, and he is a master at digging. He digs to excavate himself a little den beneath the debris on the forest floor, or to search for prey.

At the rear of this creature's jaw are two fangs. The snake uses those rear fangs to puncture prey. Why does he need to puncture his prey? This snake loves to eat frogs. When frogs are captured, they bloat up with air, so they're difficult to swallow. How do you swallow that balloon? You pop it. And that's what the snake does with his rear fangs.

I'm going to put this creature back where we found him, and let's continue searching. Let's stop in Thailand.

Here I am in the Madagascar rain forest.

See the nose?

Excellent camouflage

Bamboo viper

Have you ever seen a serpent as green as this? This is a bamboo viper, from Thailand, in Southeast Asia. It is venomous, so I have to secure it in such a way that I'm not hurting it and it's not hurting me. Amazing camouflage—the color helps this creature blend in with the foliage and teaches us that when it comes to snakes, life is easy when you're green.

This lime-green serpent is a white-lipped pit viper. As you can see by his colors, he also blends in wonderfully with the foliage in the Southeast Asian rain forest. And this animal, like 80 percent of the creatures living in this rain forest, is arboreal. That means most of his life is spent up in the treetops, moving through the branches in search of his prey.

Is he a gorgeous color?

This snake is extremely venomous, but it's not known for being very cantankerous or aggressive. With that said, I am many miles away from the nearest hospital—and I don't want this to be the last rain forest I'll explore with you as we travel around the world. So I must respect this animal and hold him very carefully. Isn't he beautiful? Notice his stocky body and arrow-shaped head. He's a stealthy hunter that just dissolves into the canopy, thanks to his color.

This snake is perfectly adaptable to the rain forest.

Speaking of green, do you remember that perfectly camouflaged vine snake we saw in Ecuador? That vine snake is native to South America. But amazingly, halfway around the world in Thailand, there is another snake, totally unrelated but identical in appearance.

Look at this perfect rain-forest snake. You can tell he's in alarm mode by the way he puffs up the front part of his body. He's spreading those green scales, exposing the white skin and the black scales. That way he looks a bit fierce, a little bit more intimidating, so you won't eat him.

Sea kraits are very, very venomous.

Guess what? I'm in Borneo. Off the coast of Borneo is a place called Snake Island—and of course there's no way I'd pass this up.

All around us are amazing and very venomous snakes. To find them, we just need to look underneath the rocks where these animals like to bury themselves.

Tucked under this rock is a yellow-lipped sea krait. These snakes are not known for being extremely aggressive, but they are very, very venomous. So I'm going to handle it as if it's hot. And when I say hot, I mean dangerous.

Sea kraits spend 90 percent of their lives in the ocean, swimming around coral reefs in search of eels, fish, and other prey. This snake is a female, and right nearby is a male. Check him out. You can see the difference between the male and the female—this guy is much smaller. They both have a large, blunt head, just like their close and equally deadly relative, the cobra.

Unlike those sea kraits from Borneo, this Southeast Asian Burmese python is not venomous. It doesn't need any venom—this snake survives by its size. It's one of the largest snakes in the world. This serpent can reach more than 20 feet

Here I am with a Burmese python friend.

in length, be as fat as a telephone pole, and weigh hundreds of pounds. And when this snake wants to eat, all it has to do is give its prey a deadly hug.

Rainbow boa

Check this out. Here's one of the prettiest constrictors living in South America, called the rainbow boa for that lustrous shine you see across its scales. It's almost glowing. You can find this animal living on the forest floor. It'll venture up into the canopy in search of birds. I want to show you something—in India.

Indian rock python

In this tree is an Indian rock python, an animal that, at one time, was very common throughout India. Today it's become increasingly rare due to habitat loss and overhunting.

This snake wasn't too happy to be taken out of her tree, but I got her. She's a moderate-sized python, a beautiful snake. She's wrapped her body around my arm. This squeeze is how she protects herself and, more importantly, how she kills her prey. My arm is turning purple because she's literally cutting off the blood flow to it. If she were hugging a baby jackal or whatever, it would be squeezed to death. Every time the animal exhaled, she would get tighter and tighter.

As cool as this python is, our trip to India has a different goal.

Let's get this snake down from her tree.

This squeeze is how the python protects itself.

I found a small village in southern India where the people, members of a tribe called the Irula, have for generations made a living finding snakes. Irula families go out to the countryside and hunt and capture venomous snakes, usually cobras. The snakes are kept in these earthen jars until they get their turn for venom extraction.

Irula snake handlers

Here we have a spectacle cobra, a very venomous snake. And he looks angry. For the venom extraction, the cobra has to be secured very carefully. Then we let him bite and eject venom naturally, just do it on his own, because we don't want to harm the snake.

Each year in India, over ten thousand people are bitten by venomous snakes. This venom will be dehydrated into a crystal and used to make antivenin, which is the medicine you use when you're bitten by a snake.

My first Russell's viper milking...

...a herpetologist's dream.

I was like a kid in a candy store in the Irula cooperative. So for my next piece of Jeff Corwin candy, I picked a Russell's viper, a snake that is extremely, extremely aggressive.

I'd never milked a Russell's viper before this, but I didn't tell them that. And I knew that this creature could be a bit testy, but I wasn't ready for the way it lashed about. We got the venom, but the snake nearly got away from me. The nature of this snake is extremely cantankerous. It's not a snake that you would ever want to mess with in the field.

A gorgeous coral snake...

...very, very venomous.

Boy, do I have a beautiful snake to show you. Just look how gorgeous it is, with those bright colors. And there's a message behind this pattern. It goes something like this: Red touches yellow, kill a fellow. Red and black, friend of Jack.

Red and yellow means this is a coral snake. I've worked with all sorts of venomous snakes, but only once have I been bitten by a venomous snake—and it was a coral. It was a message to me that I have to be real careful with venomous snakes, and I never plan on being bitten again.

This creature is the most venomous snake living in the New World. It belongs to the family we call elapids, the group that includes cobras and kraits.

Speaking of cobras, in India there's an amazing festival that's kind of like the Olympics for cobras.

Cobras are holy creatures in the Hindu religion. During the Naga Panchami festival the small town of Battis Shirala explodes with thousands of visitors who've come for one reason—cobras.

For two weeks before the festival, sixty-five teams have been collecting snakes. And now it all comes down to one final moment. There will be two winners— the team that has the fattest or heaviest snake, and the team that has the longest snake.

The cobra festival in Naga Panchami is a snake-lover's dream come true.

A cobra will only strike if its hood is extended.

Cobras everywhere

A cobra can strike out horizontally only about the same distance it can raise itself vertically. That's how these handlers know they are far enough away to be out of range of the deadly bite. This handler has a safety zone of about three feet away from his snake. The cobra will strike only when his hood is extended. These men do not fear the snakes. They believe a mutual respect between human and serpent exists. This festival, in honor of the reptile, ensures this everlasting bond.

The festival of Naga Panchami happens not only in the streets but in the households as well. In fact, it's in the house where the most important ritual takes place.

In the Hindu religion, the cobra is known as Nag. Nag is associated with Shiva, and Shiva is the god of destruction. So not only is the cobra a physically dangerous creature, it is a spiritually powerful being as well.

This is why during the festival, cobras that have been captured by expert snake handlers are treated as honored guests. In this home, the woman of the house presents a tribute to Nag, offering milk to the snake. The man of the house sprinkles vermilion powder and puts a garland over the animal's head.

Special rituals take place in the house.

A garland of red adorns this cobra.

An offering of milk is made.

45

I'm staying to enjoy the rest of the fun!

There's a lot of controversy about this festival, and I think that in an ideal world, it would be best to leave the cobras in the wild. But if you're going to have a relationship where human being and cobra come together, probably it's better that the snakes are worshiped rather than just killed out of fear.

I hope you enjoyed our journey in search of our planet's greatest snake encounters. I'll see you soon for our next adventure!

Glossary

antivenin the antidote for a snake's venom

canopy the top layer of a rain forest

constrictors snakes that kill their prey by squeezing or compression

convergence when two species in two different parts of the world evolve similar survival skills

elapid a type of venomous snake

habitat a place where animals and plants live naturally together

hemotoxin venom that damages blood and tissue

herpetologist a scientist who studies reptiles

Hindu the dominant religion in India

neurotoxin venom that damages the nervous system

ovoviviparous producing eggs that develop in the body and giving birth to live young

rain forest a tropical forest that receives a lot of rain

rostrum a snoutlike projection

serpents snakes

venomous having a gland that produces poison for self-defense or hunting

vermilion a bright red pigment

viper a type of venomous snake

Index